This Book Belongs to:

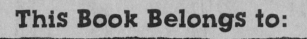

aviator

Z-Z-Z-O-O-M!

RICHARD SCARRY'S

a helicopter

ABC

WORD BOOK

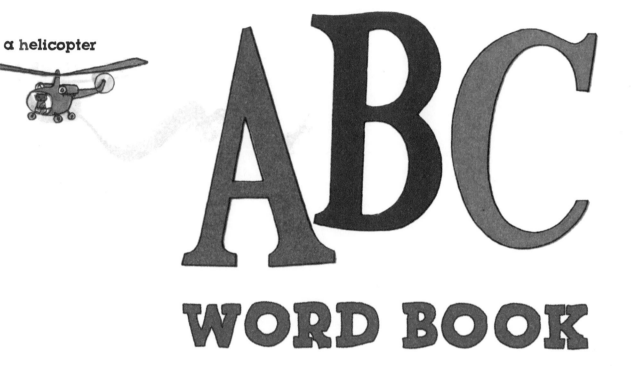

sign

DETOUR

policemen

jet plane

STERLING CHILDREN'S BOOKS
New York

An Imprint of Sterling Publishing
387 Park Avenue South
New York, NY 10016

Library of Congress Cataloging-in-Publication Data Available

Lot#:
4 6 8 10 9 7 5 3
05/15

Published by Sterling Publishing Co., Inc.
387 Park Avenue South, New York, NY 10016
www.sterlingpublishing.com/kids
By arrangement with J B Publishing, Inc.
41 River Terrace, New York, New York
On behalf of the Richard Scarry Corporation
This book was originally published in 1971.

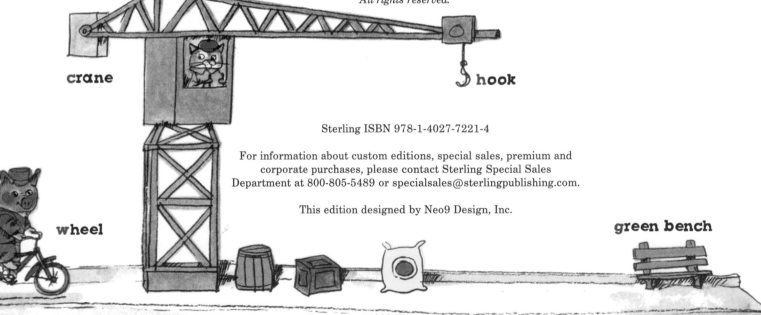

crane

hook

Sterling ISBN 978-1-4027-7221-4

For information about custom editions, special sales, premium and
corporate purchases, please contact Sterling Special Sales
Department at 800-805-5489 or specialsales@sterlingpublishing.com.

This edition designed by Neo9 Design, Inc.

wheel

green bench

RICHARD SCARRY'S

ABC

WORD BOOK

parachute

bridge

car

BARBER

mouse

fisherman

yacht

submarine

STERLING CHILDREN'S BOOKS

New York

Aa

As Mother Cat was driving Father Cat to the airport, she had an accident.

vintage car

policeman

crane

tow truck on the way to an accident

ambulance

taxi

hydrant

arm

umbrella

GAS STATION

attendant

cane

farmer

hat

hay cart

a racing car going fast

tractor

MAIL

AIR MAIL

SANITATION TRUCK

The sanitation worker has a flat tire. He is sad.

flat tire

jack

sack of potatoes

bag of asparagus

DANGER

basket of apples

traffic signal

manhole

ABC FARM

CRASH!

car

farm truck

PARKING

baby carriage

No one was hurt in the accident because everybody was wearing a seatbelt.

sidewalk

A a

wind vane

hangar

tail

stewardess

boarding stairs

traveler

Father Cat

FOLLOW ME

a flat rabbit

At the airport a plane
is about to land all alone.
The aviator is landing
by parachute.

Hilda is running out
of the way to safety.

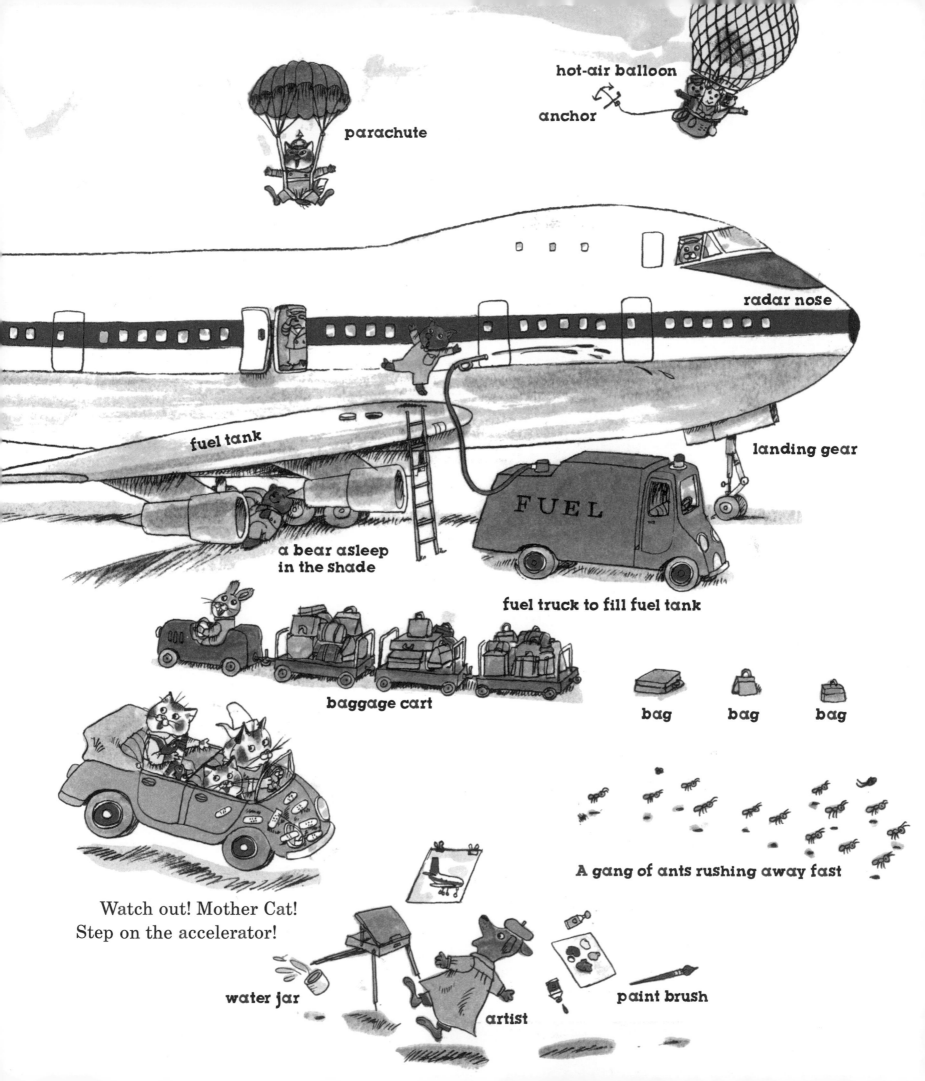

parachute

hot-air balloon

anchor

radar nose

fuel tank

landing gear

a bear asleep
in the shade

fuel truck to fill fuel tank

baggage cart

bag   bag   bag

A gang of ants rushing away fast

Watch out! Mother Cat!
Step on the accelerator!

water jar

artist

paint brush

Bb

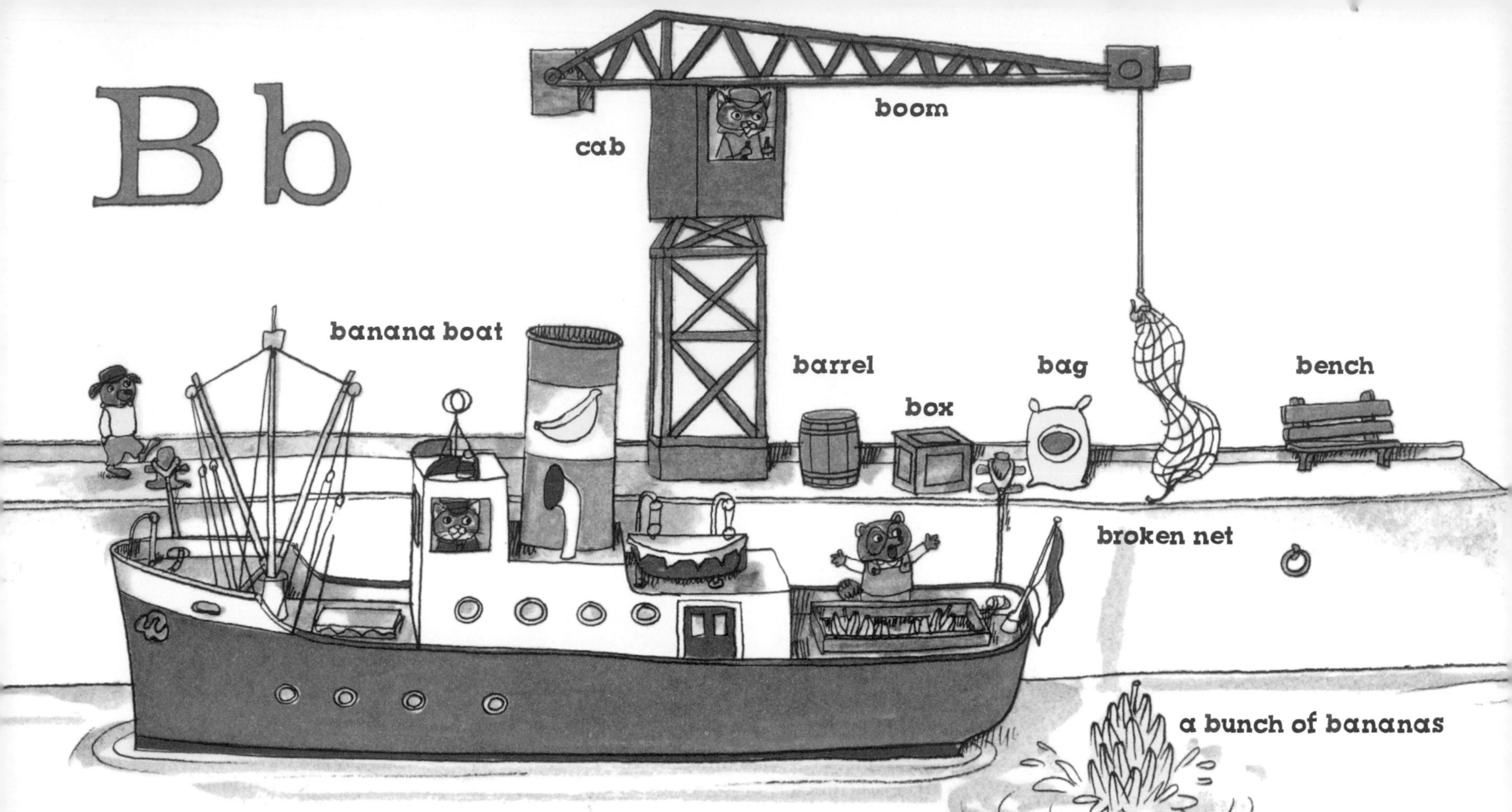

cab

boom

banana boat

barrel

box

bag

bench

broken net

a bunch of bananas

My, what a busy harbor
with boats all about.

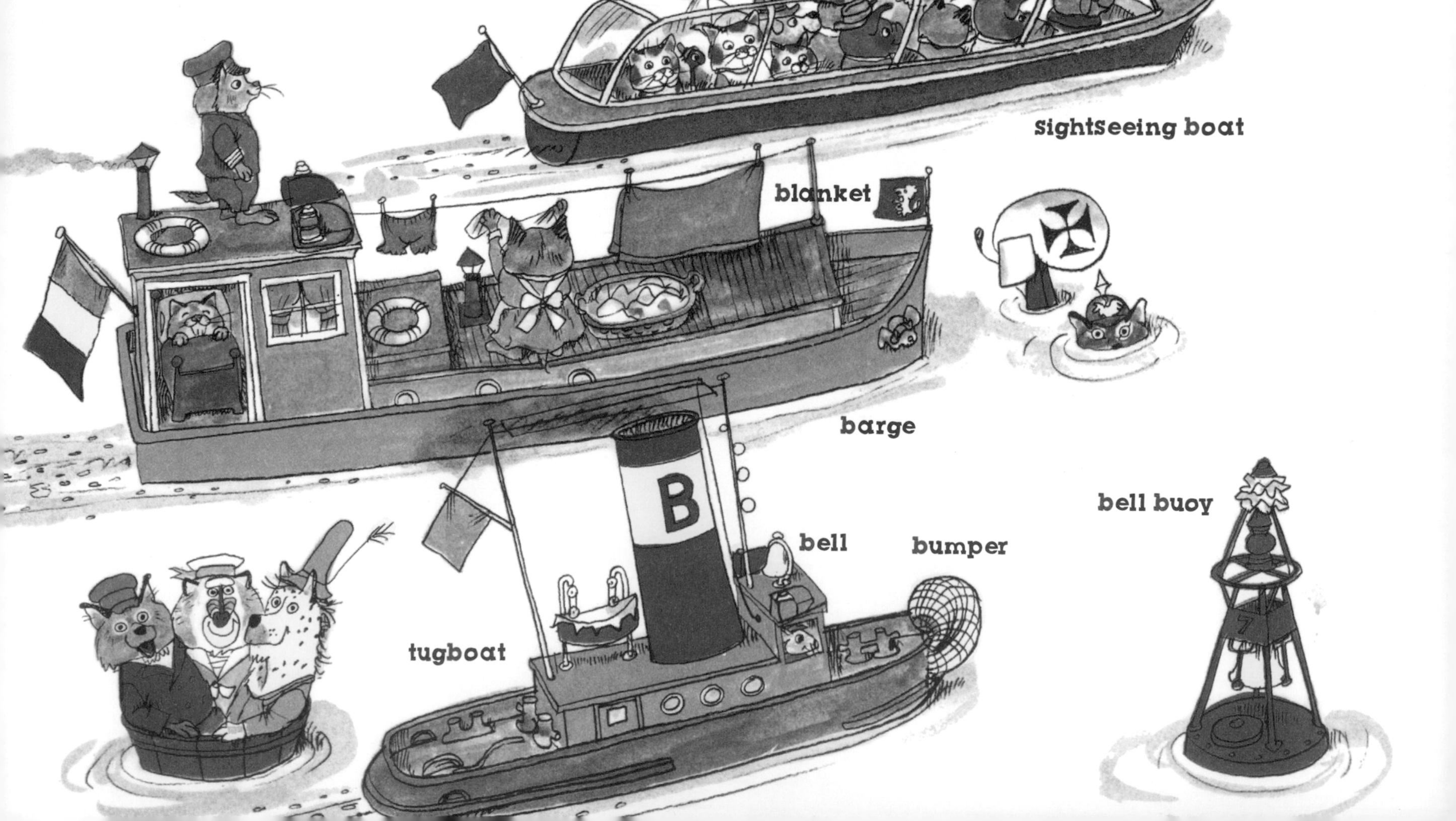

sightseeing boat

blanket

barge

bell buoy

bell

bumper

tugboat

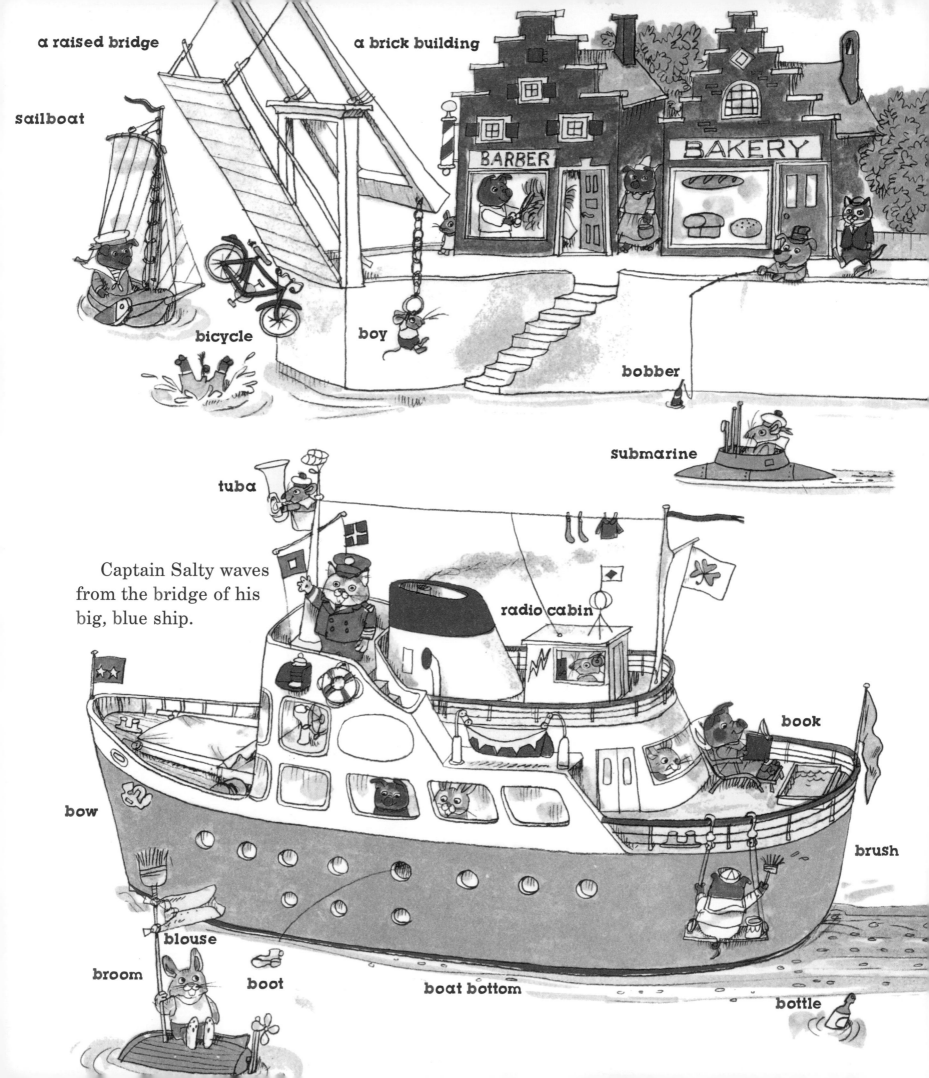

a raised bridge

a brick building

sailboat

BARBER

BAKERY

bicycle

boy

bobber

submarine

tuba

Captain Salty waves
from the bridge of his
big, blue ship.

radio cabin

book

bow

brush

blouse

broom

boot

boat bottom

bottle

Cc

A crowd came to Tiger Cat's picnic. Everyone licked ice-cream cones and danced to the lively music.

ice-cream cone

cup

A couple of mice served cider from a cement mixer.

a cook's cap

Tiger Cat cooked popcorn. The cover wasn't closed. ***Crackle! Crackle! Pop!*** Be careful, Tiger Cat!

coffeepot

cover

camp stove

POP CORN

can

can opener

Rudolf cracked up.

cornet

camera

Crab caught popcorn
in his claws.

accordion

Lowly danced in a circle
with a piece of celery.

candle

Clarence couldn't count
the biscuits that he ate.

Curly Pig accidentally fell into
the center of the cake. **CRASH!**

What a crazy, cuckoo picnic!

Ch ch

church steeple

It is a chilly day, but everyone is
full of good cheer. Christmas is tomorrow!
The bells chime in the church steeple.

church

A chimney sweep
scratching his
itchy chin

CHOICE
and
CHEAP
MEAT
CHARLES CHIMP

The yule log is attached
to the sled with a chain.

latch

chickens

butcher

chimney

children caroling

kerchief

patch

Ma Pig is chatting with Mrs. Chipmunk.
She is also burning the chop for her
children's lunch.
    She is a champion chatterbox.

china

chair

stitch

match

bench

wristwatch

D d

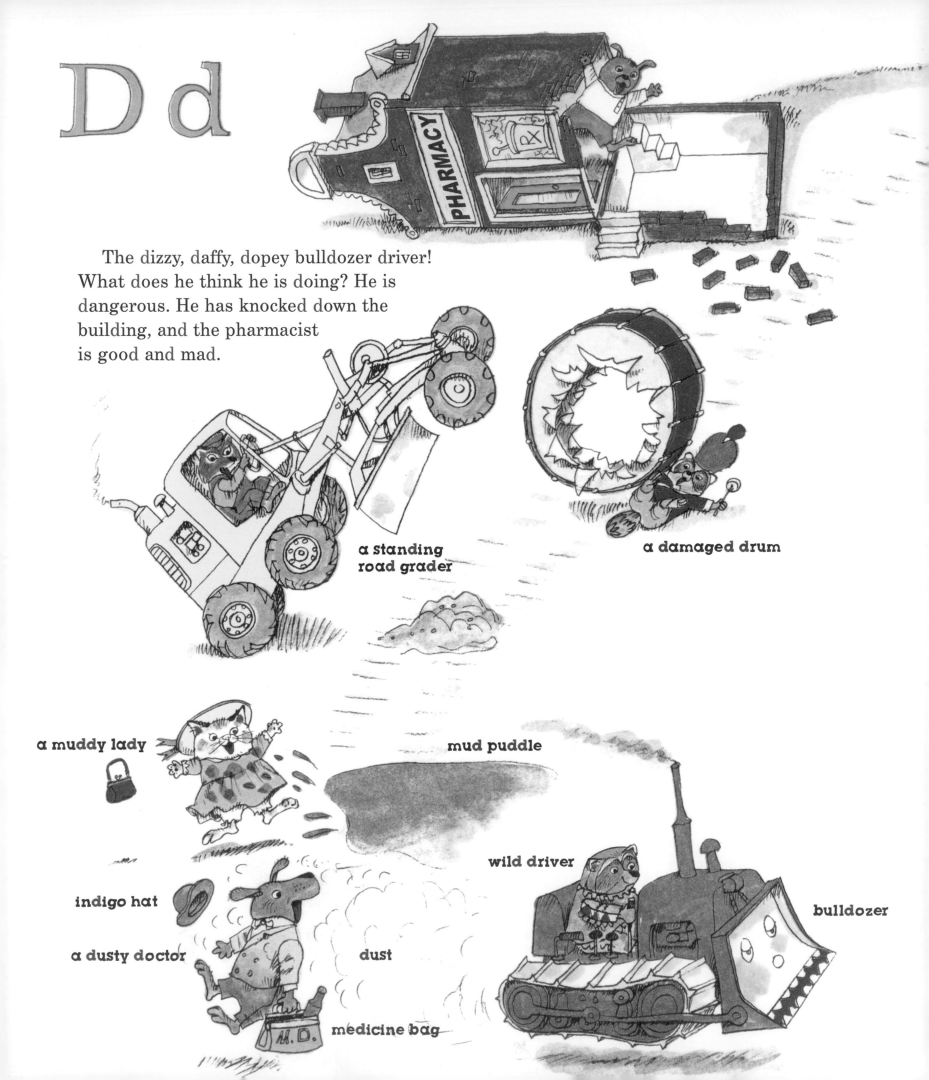

The dizzy, daffy, dopey bulldozer driver! What does he think he is doing? He is dangerous. He has knocked down the building, and the pharmacist is good and mad.

a standing road grader

a damaged drum

a muddy lady

mud puddle

wild driver

indigo hat

bulldozer

a dusty doctor

dust

medicine bag

DETOUR

a dumped-over
dump truck

dirt

derrick

board

a scared ditch-digger

Where
is Huckle
hiding?

drill

ladder

door

DANGER

a dozen
doughnuts

delivery man

a deep ditch

DOUGHNUTS

E e

Ernie Elephant and his excellent firemen
have just driven up to extinguish an enormous
fire. Mother Rabbit is screaming for help.
Do not fear! They will save her.

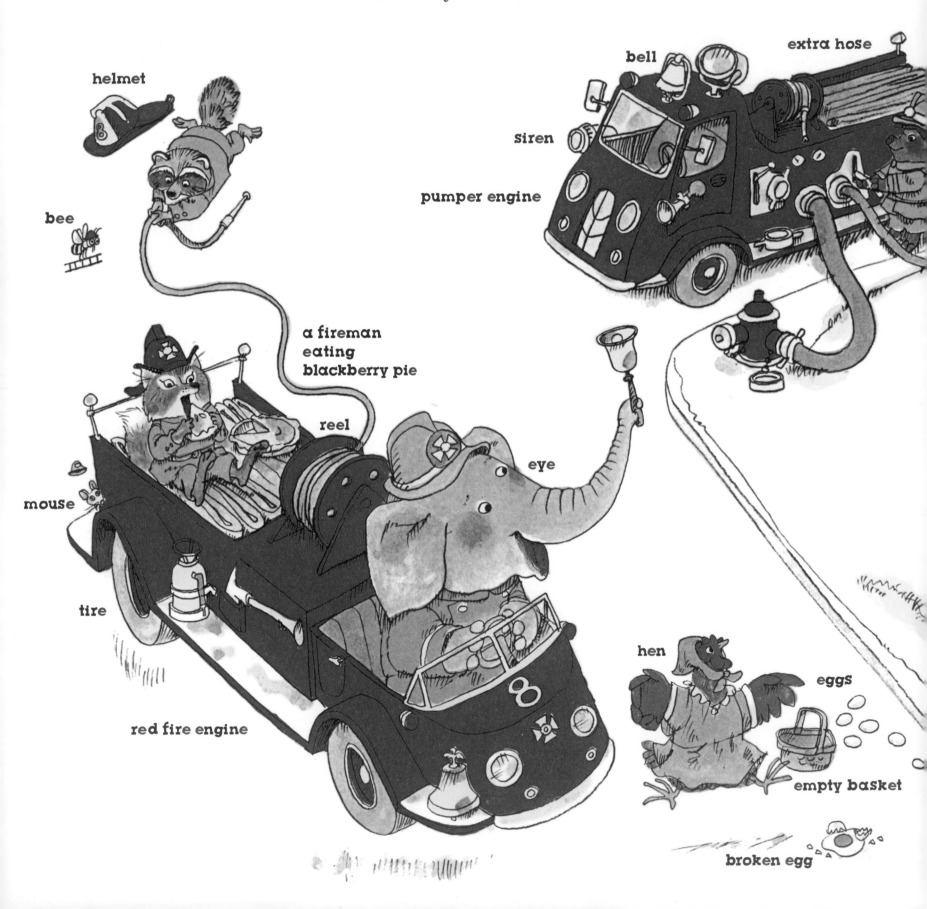

helmet

bee

a fireman
eating
blackberry pie

reel

mouse

tire

red fire engine

extra hose

bell

siren

pumper engine

eye

hen

eggs

empty basket

broken egg

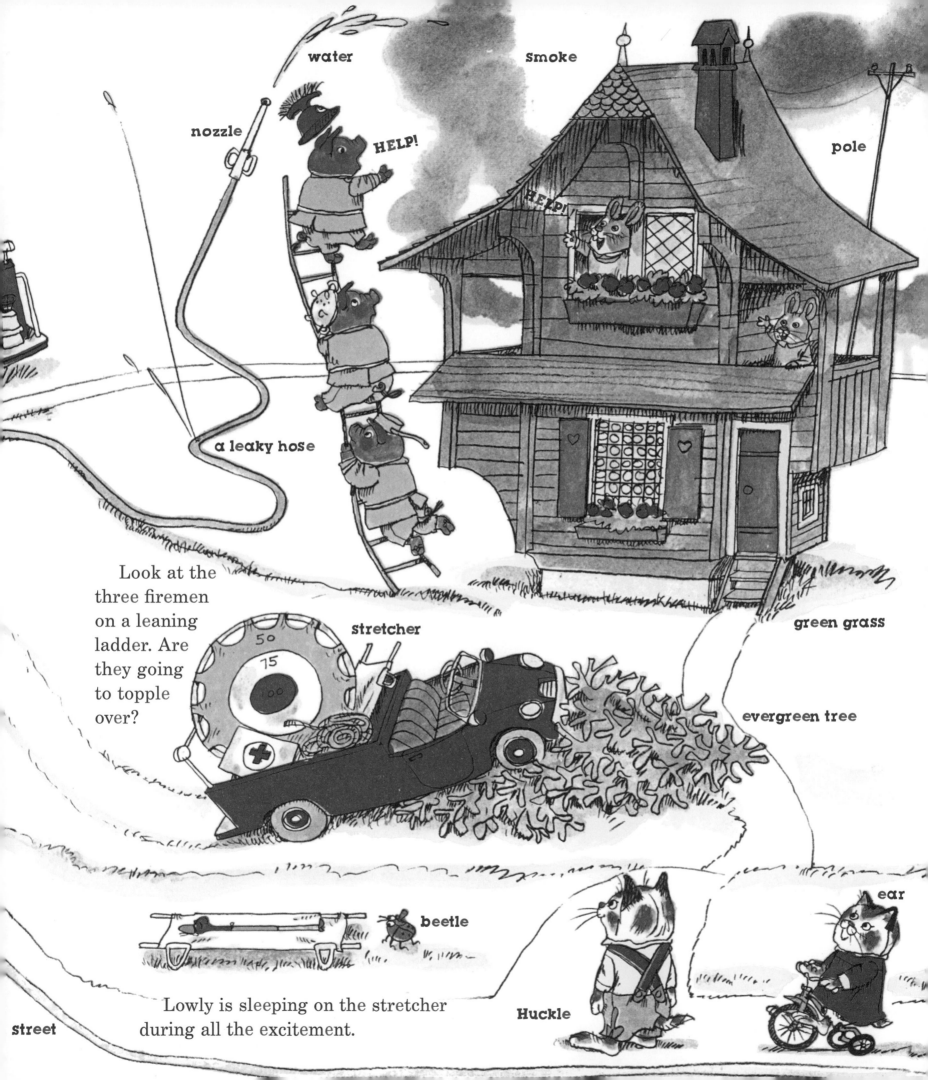

water

smoke

nozzle

HELP!

HELP!

pole

a leaky hose

Look at the three firemen on a leaning ladder. Are they going to topple over?

stretcher

green grass

evergreen tree

beetle

ear

Lowly is sleeping on the stretcher during all the excitement.

Huckle

street

F f

giraffe

leaf

a fast freight train

a fruit tree

fertilizer

fence

Farmer Fox grows food
in his fields for his family.
There are five furry foxes
hiding in the farmhouse.
Can you find them?

field

front wheels

three frankfurters

a funny face

flag

farmhouse roof

forest

flower

flow

fireplace

muffins

flames

flour

floor

one fly

Five flies follow each other in a single file.

a fat fish

Huckle fell flat on his face.

foot

four fish

Wolf and his friend Freddy Frog

knife

a floating cap

G g

What is going on at Greasy George's garage?

GREASY GEORGE'S GORGEOUS GARAGE

a great big green fuel truck

GOOD GAS

girl

green gas pump

GOOD GAS

bag

grill

hot dog

a guitar string

Goofy Goose is going to take a group of gabby goslings to the picnic grounds. Ugh! He is groaning at the thought.

GO RIGHT

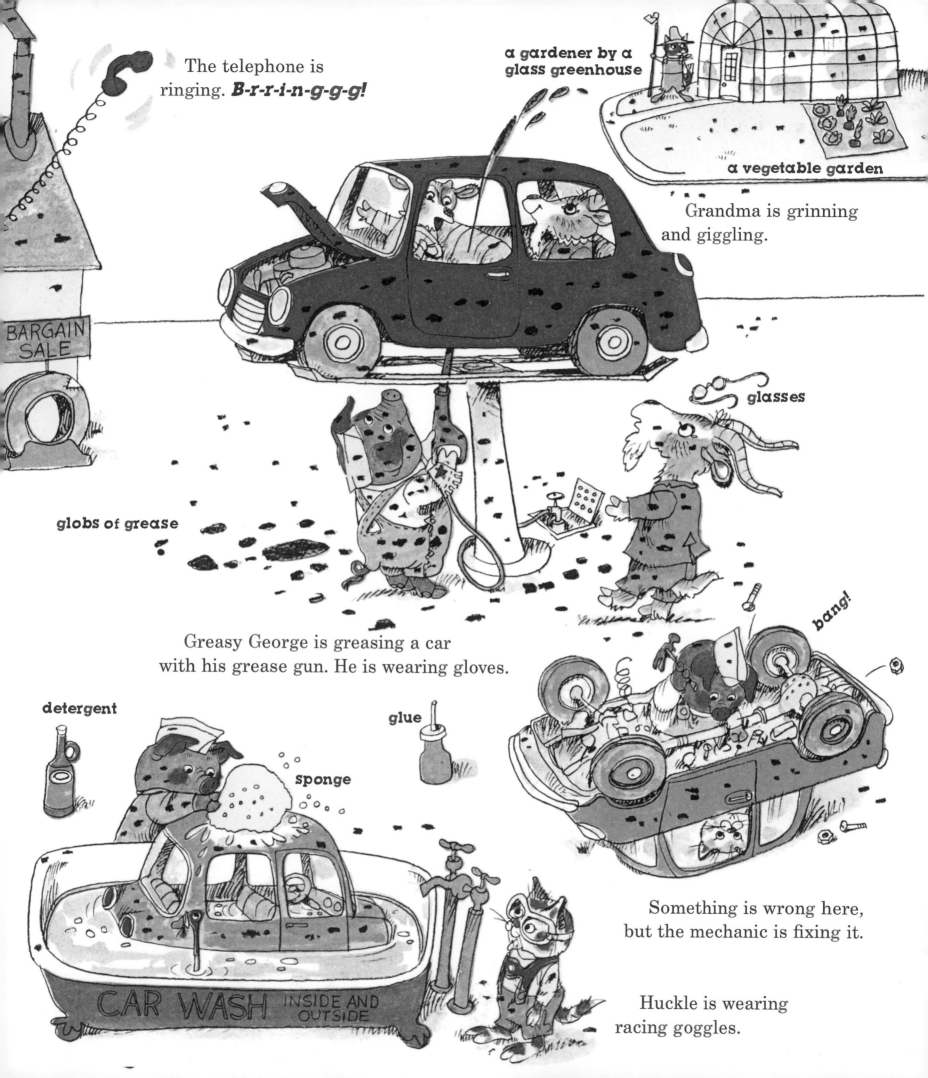

The telephone is ringing. **B-r-r-i-n-g-g-g!**

a gardener by a glass greenhouse

a vegetable garden

Grandma is grinning and giggling.

BARGAIN SALE

glasses

globs of grease

Greasy George is greasing a car with his grease gun. He is wearing gloves.

detergent

glue

sponge

bang!

Something is wrong here, but the mechanic is fixing it.

CAR WASH INSIDE AND OUTSIDE

Huckle is wearing racing goggles.

H h

Here is a happy home.
However, someone is unhappy.
Father hired a helper to fix
the roof shingles and the helper
hit his thumb with the hammer.
"OUCH!" he howled.

a head poking through a hole in a hat

heart

shutter

children

hatchet

hoe

Ha-ha!

hose

Huckle has a *very* high hat
on his head and a horn in
his hands. He is blowing hard.

a hard rock

a helicopter hovering
high above the earth

a tree house

branch

Someone is hiding
in a heap of clothes.

hook

hanger

hot water

shower

Hurry, Mother! Something is
happening to the spaghetti.

pitcher

honey

dish   ketchup

a hen in a hurry

bush

shovel

Father is digging a hole
in which to plant a bush.

wheelbarrow

hole

I i

It is a very windy day. The sails of the windmill were spinning around fast until Uncle Irving's kite string tied them up. The miller is furious. He has an important order to fill.

Rudolf's diving high-flyer lost its wings in flight. Rudolf is going swimming with his friends.

a high hill

pipe

Willy, a little pig, is licking an ice-cream cone and spilling it on Uncle Irving's shirt.

wire fence

cliff

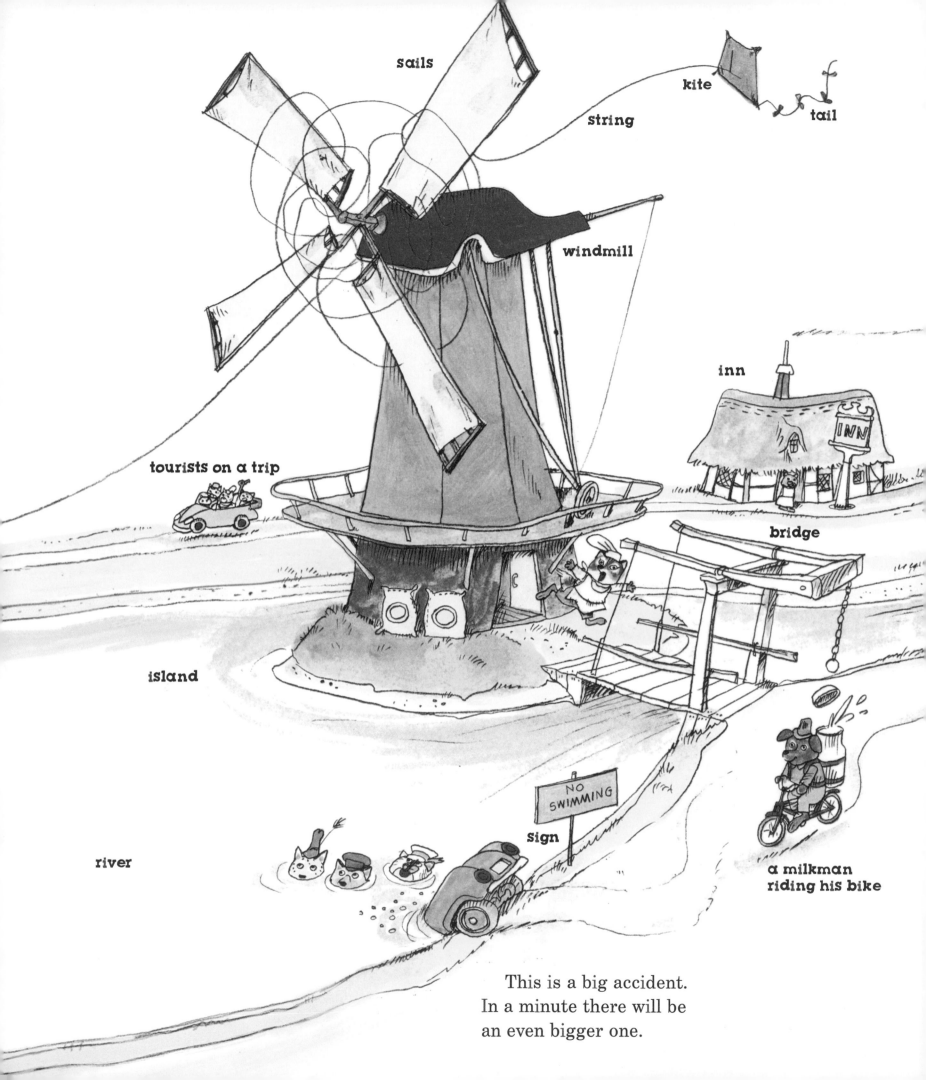

sails

kite

string

tail

windmill

inn

tourists on a trip

bridge

island

NO SWIMMING

sign

river

a milkman riding his bike

This is a big accident.
In a minute there will be
an even bigger one.

J j

jungle gym

Hilda just jammed a grapefruit
between her jaws and went **c-r-u-n-c-h.**
Was it juicy, Hilda?

jaw

jewel

jumping Jill

pajamas

jug

jack-o'-lantern

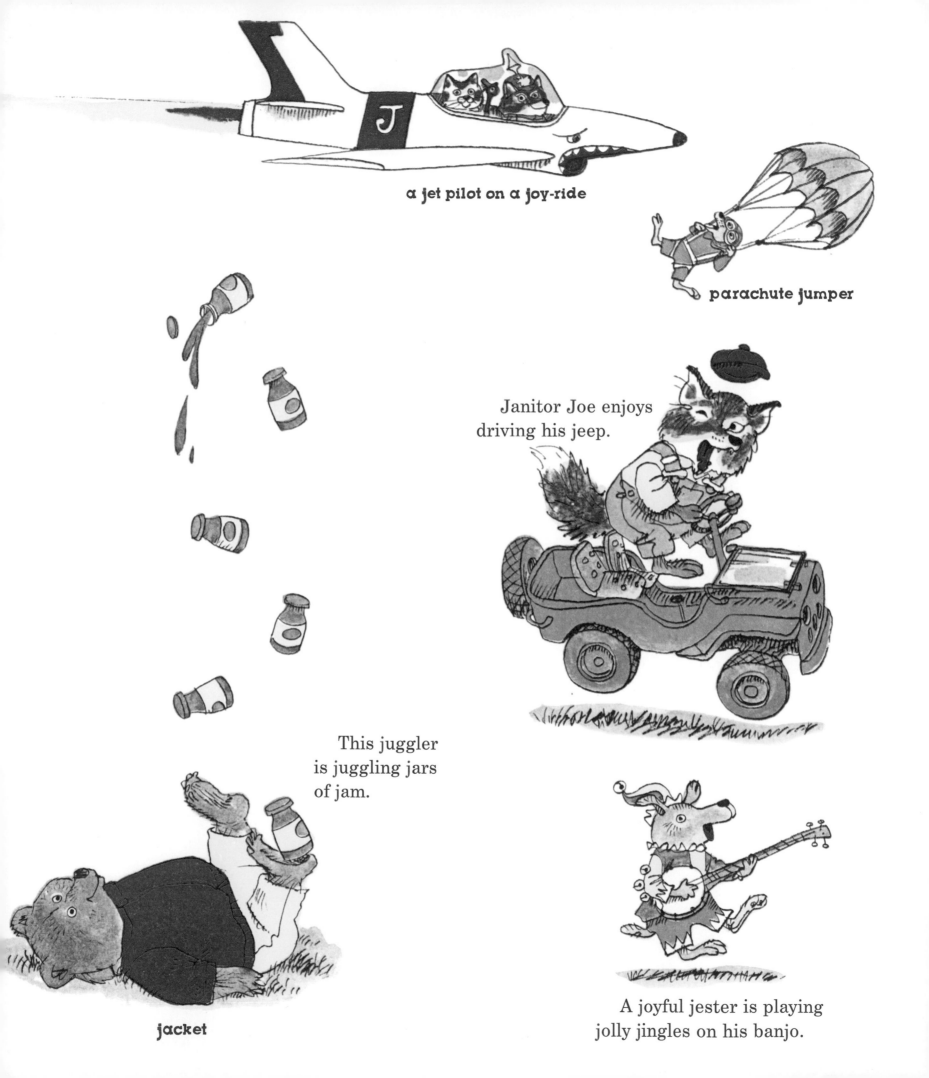

a jet pilot on a joy-ride

parachute jumper

Janitor Joe enjoys driving his jeep.

This juggler is juggling jars of jam.

jacket

A joyful jester is playing jolly jingles on his banjo.

K k

The king is having a snack.
He is licking a gherkin.
Kangaroo is skating in with
a cake she has baked for the king.
Would you like to share his snack?

a turkey soaking
in the sink

Duck likes to drink milk.

king

gherkin

napkin

fork

key

pocket

baked bricks

a basket of crackers

broken leg

sock

Kitten is sucking
milk through a straw.

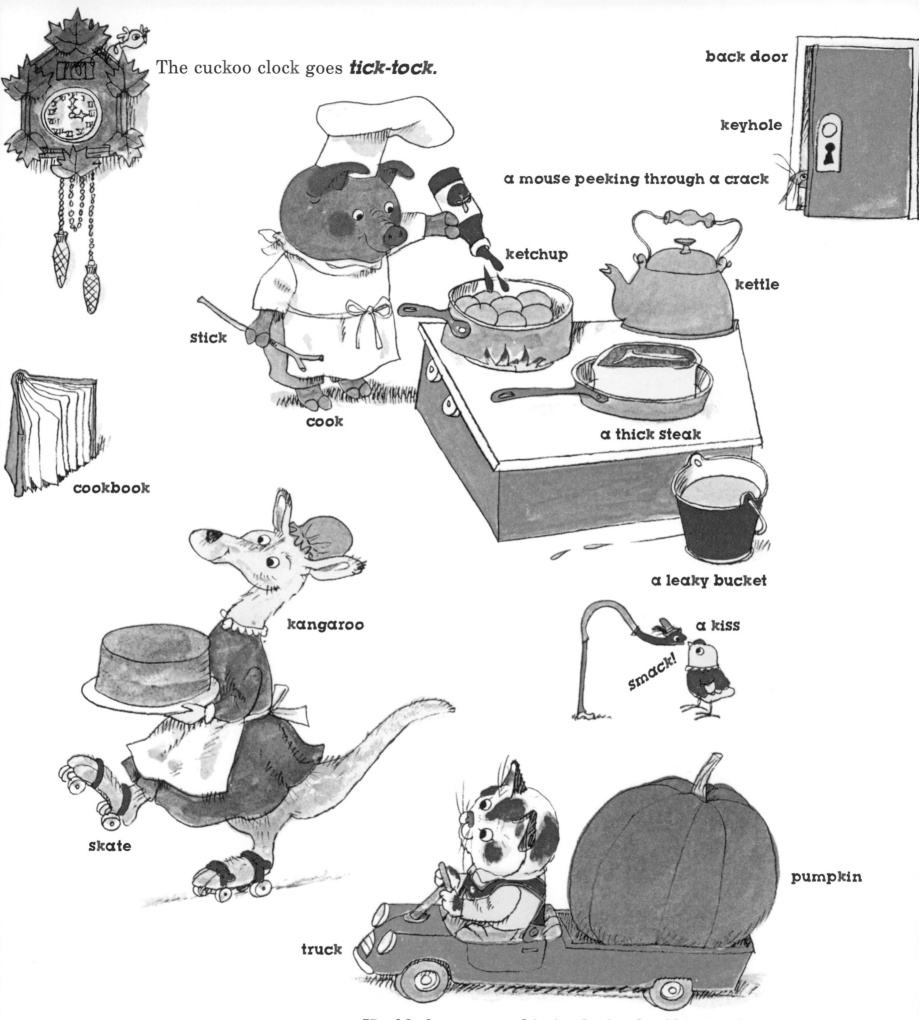

The cuckoo clock goes **tick-tock.**

back door

keyhole

a mouse peeking through a crack

ketchup

kettle

stick

cook

a thick steak

cookbook

a leaky bucket

kangaroo

a kiss

smack!

skate

pumpkin

truck

Huckle has a pumpkin in the back of his truck.

L l

A large steamroller is rolling wildly over the land. Look out, all you people, or you will be flattened!

a leaning sign

a flat limousine

The postman slipped and lost a lot of letters.

MAIL

a flat bicycle

a flat lawn mower

towel

a little girl licking a lollipop

leapfrog

Mrs. Pig is losing her clean laundry. She calls out loudly, "Let go of my laundry! And please leave my lovely flowers alone."

oil barrel

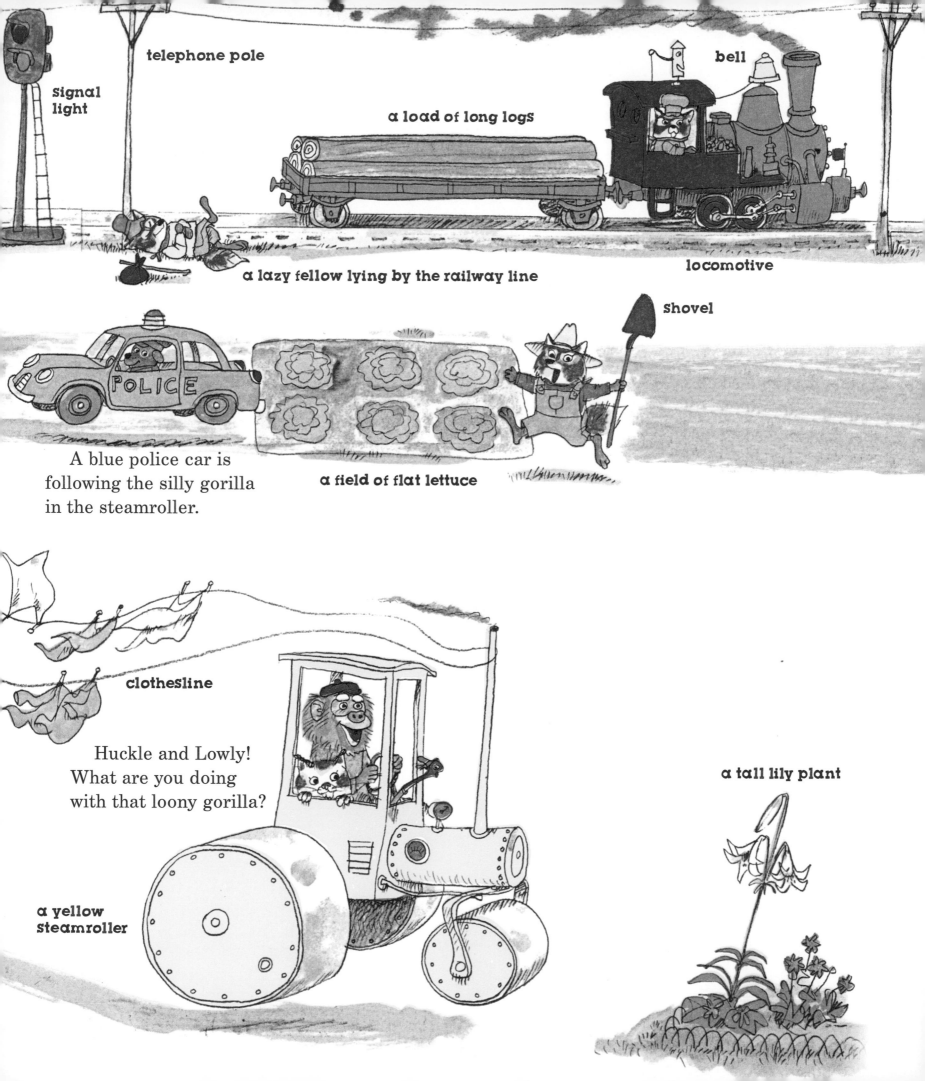

signal
light

telephone pole

bell

a load of long logs

locomotive

a lazy fellow lying by the railway line

shovel

A blue police car is
following the silly gorilla
in the steamroller.

a field of flat lettuce

clothesline

Huckle and Lowly!
What are you doing
with that loony gorilla?

a tall lily plant

a yellow
steamroller

Mm

mouse

drum

trombone

merry firemen making music

cement mixer

ambulance

medicine

instruments

ice-cream man

bump!

Doctor Monday on a bumpy road

ICE CREAM

mail truck

milk truck

bumper

mirror

monument

motorcycle

WILLIAM TELL

PLUMBER

smoke

plumber's truck

Something is the matter with Mommy's motor. A mechanic is trying to make it go.

Father Pig is stuck in the messy, muddy road. How mad he is! Oh, my!

a messy, muddy road

SPEED LIMIT 60 M.P.H.

Nn

airplane

orange crane

nose

Rudolf's plane landed in a pond.
A crane yanked it out.

a broken fence

net

a bunch of bananas

a nice nursemaid and
an infant napping

HIGH STREET

another runner
in pink pants

a policeman running

sign

nine pine trees in a long truck

TREE
NURSER

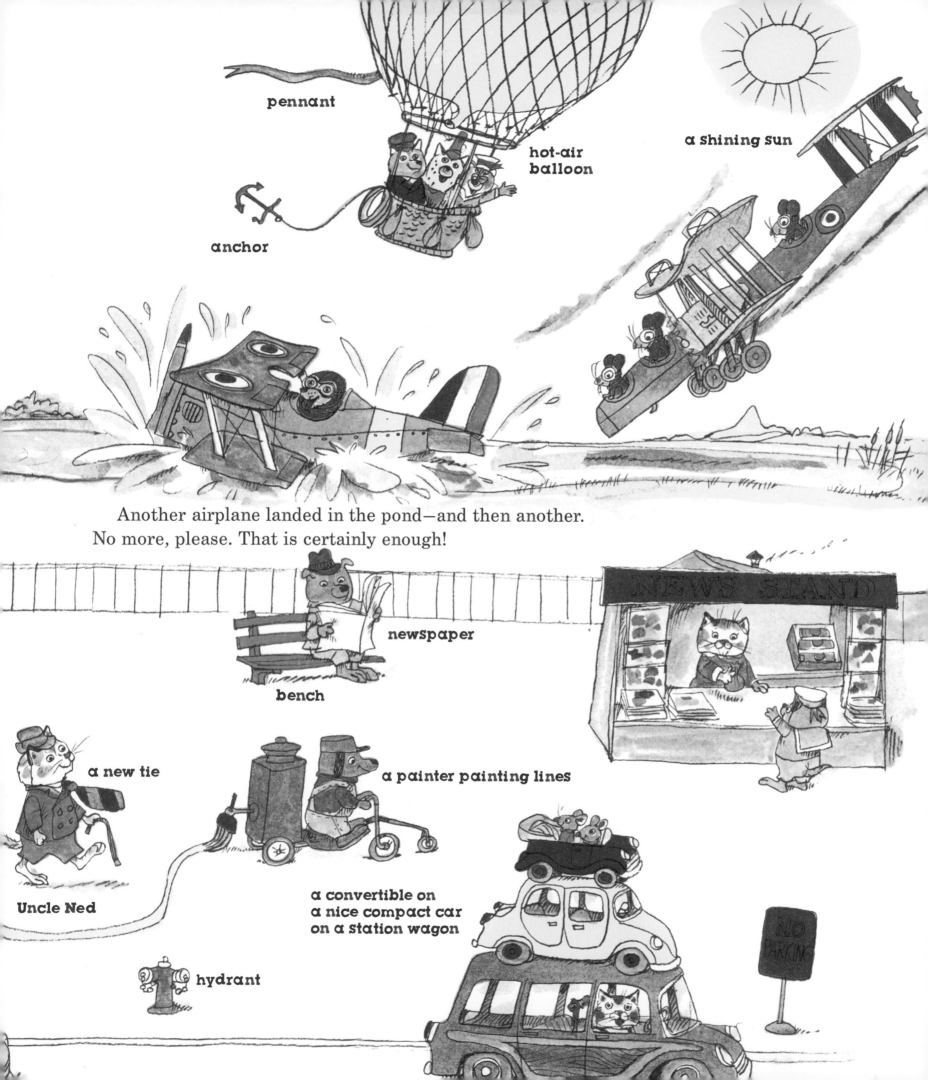

pennant

hot-air
balloon

a shining sun

anchor

Another airplane landed in the pond—and then another.
No more, please. That is certainly enough!

newspaper

bench

NEWS STAND

a new tie

a painter painting lines

Uncle Ned

a convertible on
a nice compact car
on a station wagon

hydrant

NO PARKING

Oo

Oh, my! See how many people have come down to the harbor to see the boats dock.

lookout

boy

boat

toot!

horn

pilot house

Captain Fox

hello!

bow

portholes

Sailor Dog overboard!

rose

rowboat

oar

octopus

good-bye!

codfish

boots

sole

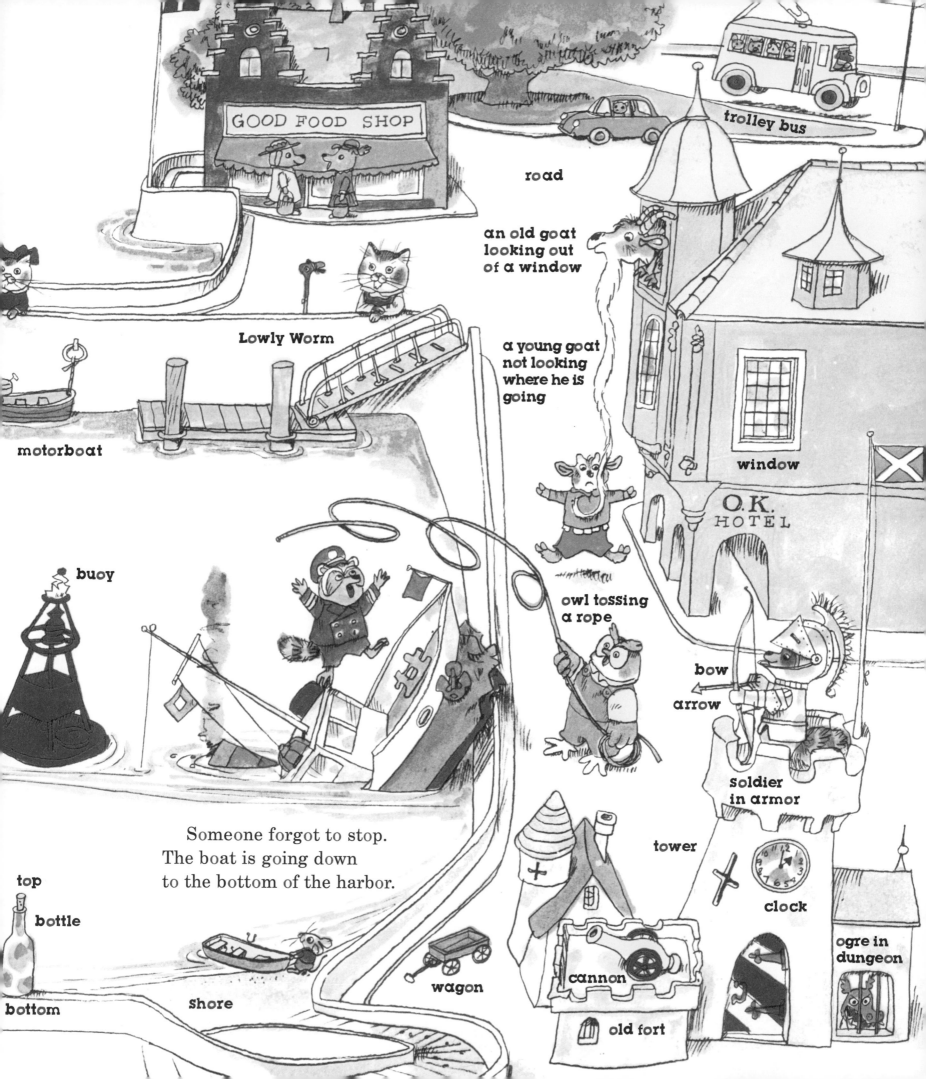

GOOD FOOD SHOP

road

trolley bus

an old goat looking out of a window

Lowly Worm

a young goat not looking where he is going

window

motorboat

O.K. HOTEL

buoy

owl tossing a rope

bow

arrow

soldier in armor

Someone forgot to stop.
The boat is going down
to the bottom of the harbor.

tower

top

bottle

clock

bottom

shore

wagon

cannon

ogre in dungeon

old fort

P p

Pretty Polly Pig is having a party.
She is playing the piano. *Plink! Plink!*
All the people are happy.

trumpet

pin

palm tree

piano

pot

plaid

bagpipe

platform

piccolo

Porcupine goes
poo-poo-pa-do
on his saxophone.

sharp points

pelican eating peanuts

penguin

present

parrot

puffin

peach

pineapple

pear

a person
peeling apples
up in a lamp

plate

Peter is pushing
Paul. Stop that, Peter.
Don't be a pest!

carpet

a group of pigs

Huckle slips and
drops the plum pudding.
Lowly jumps up and
catches it.
  Put it back on
the plate, Lowly!

Little Sister
pours pink punch
from a pint jug
into a paper cup.
Don't spill, please.

punch bowl

plop!

teapot

pie

Q q

The queen is playing croquet with her friends.
They seem to be quarreling. Please! Let's be quiet!

squeak!

squeak!

squeal!

squeal!

quack!

quack!

squaw

The queen in her quilted robe

Two squirrels are playing a quick game of ring toss.

Quincy squeezes his water gun and water squirts out.

It hits a squid in his aquarium.

Quit it!

Quite a nice shot, Queenie!

Two girls play hopscotch on numbered squares.

mosquito

a quart of milk

Rr

rabbit ear

G-r-r-r!

rudder

racing boat

pirate

raft

The Rapid Rabbits were racing the River Rascals in a rowing race up the river. The steersman steered right onto a rock. **C-r-u-n-c-h!**

The race was over. He was in a furious rage.

drowning Lowly Worm

Huckle rescuing a swimmer

Bravo!

umbrella

Rhinoceros is rather peculiar. He prefers not to get wet when he goes into the water.

raincoat

reeds

a hungry beggar wearing rags

rubber boots

ribbon

radio

a tired rower resting

carrot

rock

the losers

the winners

A rooster can crow.
Can a crow rooster?

rope

water ski

raccoon

THREE STAR
RESTAURANT

REST
ROOM

A waiter is carrying a tray of fruit to
a customer. Who left that chair where
someone would surely trip over it?

very bad
manners

S s

brush

smack!

stilts

scooter

Daddy Pig came into the house and kissed Mommy.
"What's for supper?" he asked.

"Your seven silly cousins are visiting us for
several days," answered Mommy. "They wish
to cook and serve our meals to us. They are
making a super surprise supper now."

"Something does smell delicious," said Daddy.
"Let's see what it is that smells so good."

Oh! Such a sight they saw!

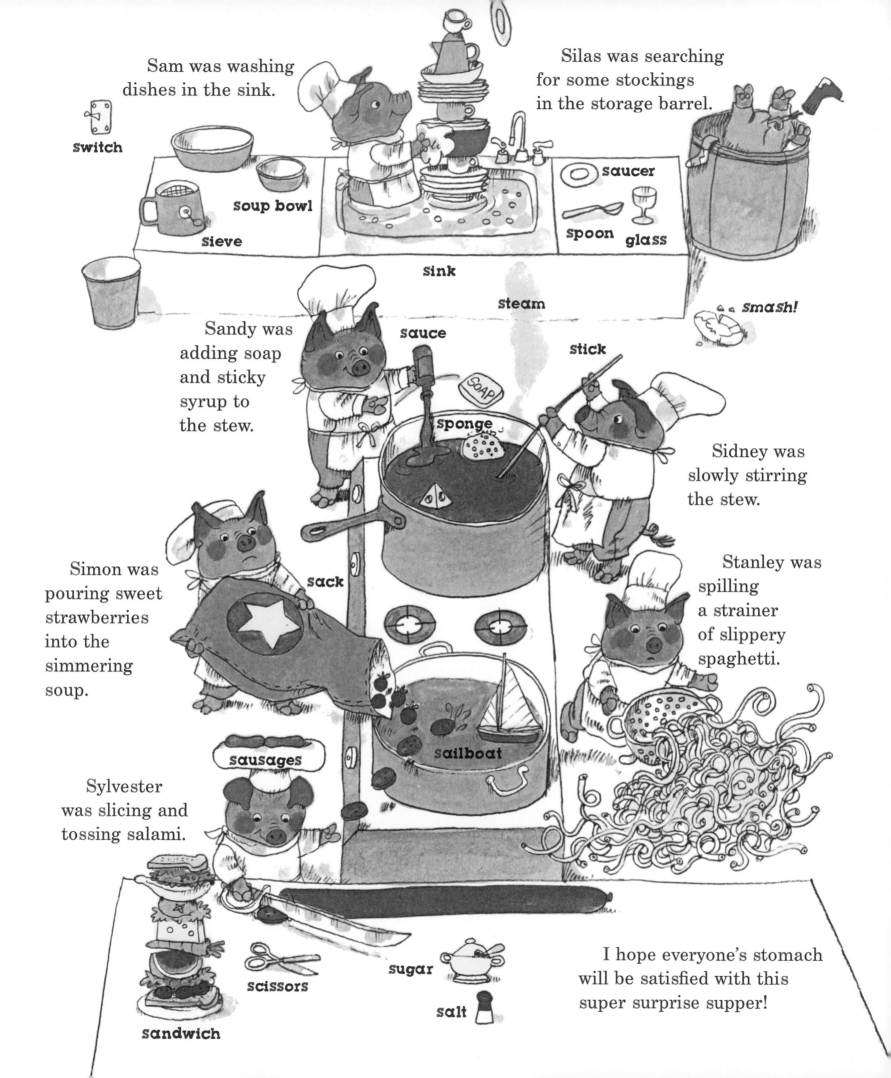

Sam was washing dishes in the sink.

Silas was searching for some stockings in the storage barrel.

switch

soup bowl

sieve

saucer

spoon **glass**

sink

steam

smash!

Sandy was adding soap and sticky syrup to the stew.

sauce

stick

sponge

SOAP

Sidney was slowly stirring the stew.

Simon was pouring sweet strawberries into the simmering soup.

sack

Stanley was spilling a strainer of slippery spaghetti.

sausages

sailboat

Sylvester was slicing and tossing salami.

scissors

sugar

salt

sandwich

I hope everyone's stomach will be satisfied with this super surprise supper!

Sh sh

shade

shaving brush

shelf

a shoulder shawl

wash tub

shoe

What a shame! Mother Bear washed a shirt, and it shrank. Father Bear is blushing with embarrassment.

washing-line

a sheet with shapes shaking inside it

shell

sharp shears

a shaggy mop

shampoo

splish!

splash!

splash!

splosh!

shower

mashed potatoes

A sheep in shabby clothes crashed through
the door to show what his brushes could do.
One could even turn on the shower!
Mother told him to shut the door.
The cold air was making her shiver.

Children were dashing and
rushing about, shrieking and
shouting, pushing and shoving.
Hush, shildren! Be shilent!
I mean, Hush, children! Be silent!

T t

Take a look at the terrible accident.
A train has hit a truck that contained
ten thousand tomatoes. What a sight!

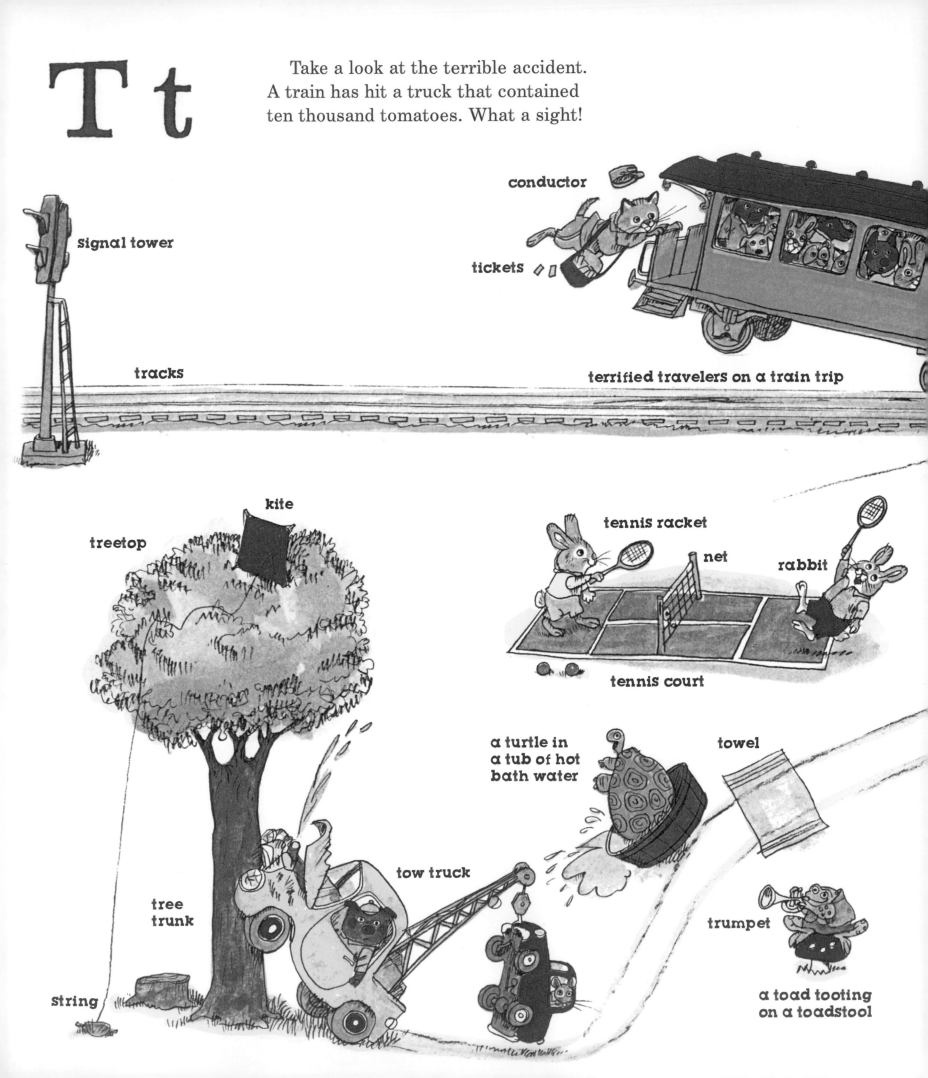

conductor

signal tower

tickets

tracks

terrified travelers on a train trip

kite

treetop

tennis racket

net

rabbit

tennis court

a turtle in
a tub of hot
bath water

towel

tow truck

tree
trunk

trumpet

string

a toad tooting
on a toadstool

smokestack

tomatoes

tires

tennis ball

a crossing gate torn in two

truck

tent

pot

street

tire tracks

television set

lantern

Little Sister riding her tricycle

table

tepee

Rudolf returned to earth too fast and left a great
rut in the dirt. Look! You're on television, Rudolf!

rut

Th th

King Theodore Thaddeus walked down the path without thinking whither he was going. He walked into a thicket of thistles.

thistles

Thrashing about, he found he was stuck to them. *This*, he thought, *is a terrible thing!* Then he threw off his thick cloth suit, and in three seconds he was free.

However, the weather was cold, and all he had on were thin underthings. It is not healthy to wear nothing but that in the cold.

scythe

Just then Thelma, a nice lady, came along.
"WHAT ON EARTH!" she said. "Something must be done."

She cut some straw with her scythe.
Then she put a thimble on her thumb,
and with her needle and thread she made
Theodore Thaddeus a new suit of straw thatch.
King Theodore Thaddeus thanked Thelma
a thousand times.

They went back to his castle together,
and sat within the hearth.
    Then King Theodore Thaddeus thought . . .
Why not?
    Right then and there he asked Thelma to be
his queen and share his throne with him.
    Thelma was breathless. Nevertheless . . .
she said "YES!"
    What do you think of that!

hearth

Uu

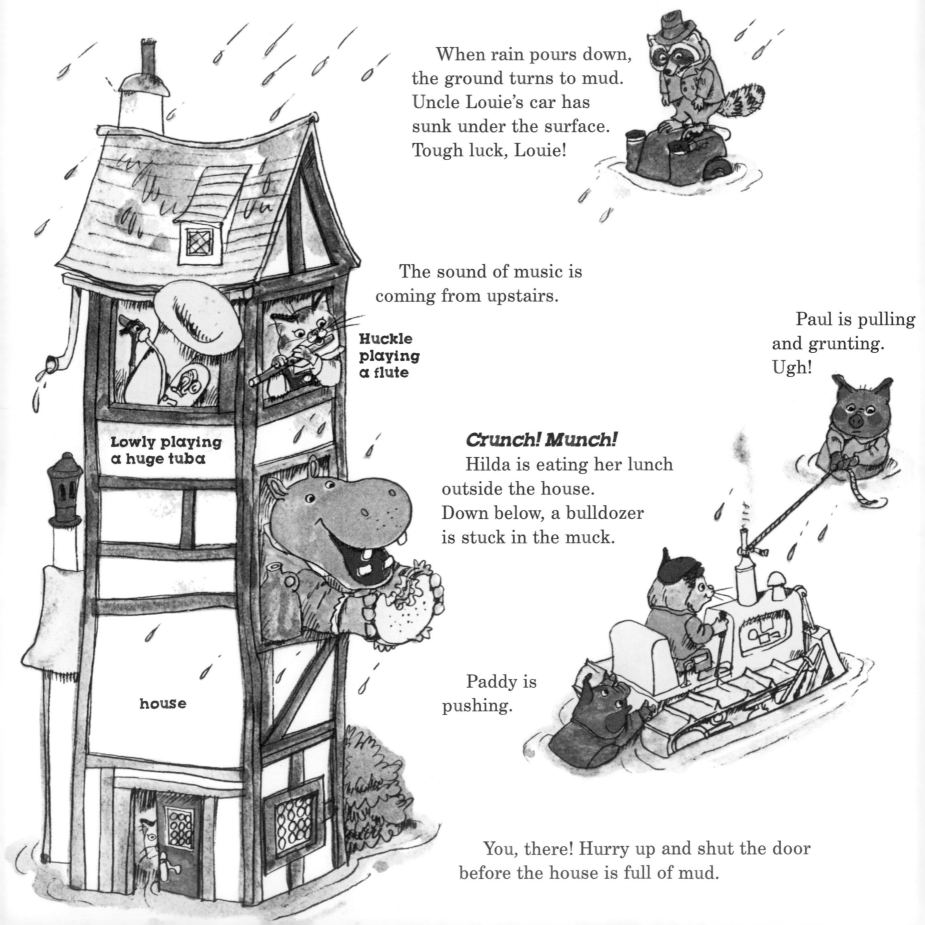

When rain pours down, the ground turns to mud. Uncle Louie's car has sunk under the surface. Tough luck, Louie!

The sound of music is coming from upstairs.

Paul is pulling and grunting. Ugh!

Huckle playing a flute

Lowly playing a huge tuba

Crunch! Munch!
Hilda is eating her lunch outside the house. Down below, a bulldozer is stuck in the muck.

house

Paddy is pushing.

You, there! Hurry up and shut the door before the house is full of mud.

underwear

Even Rudolf has put up his umbrella. Too bad he is upside down.

BUTCHER

Aunt Ursula is jumping home after buying enough sausages for supper.

Duck is busy unloading nuts out of his dump truck.

nuts

FOURTH AVENUE

Sergeant Murphy is shouting loudly, "Don't clutter up the avenue!"

a muddy uniform

V v

aviator

glove

weather vane

A vintage car is driving through a village and over a very high viaduct. This roving family is going to visit relatives.

VILLAGE OF LOVE

two chatting wives

viaduct

a van with five jugs of vinegar

a driver

river

a brave cat diving to save a mouse

violets

volcano

grape vines

Vincent lives in
a cave. He is shaving
his lovely face.

a jolly violin player

Victor, the Viking, is arriving home
in his sailing vessel after a very long voyage.

W w

The weather is wild and windy.
The whole town is blowing away.

wig

walrus

a window washer
wiping a window

Lowly Worm
inside a watermelon

water

a waiter losing
his warm stew

Wait!

paw

wristwatch

Wolf howling at
his hat

Huckle is wearing
a weight to hold
him down.

a whirring, twirling windmill

a wet towel

a wool sweater

woods

Owl growing wheat in a meadow

a girl watching at the window

wrench

a witch in a wheelbarrow

a new wooden wagon

wheel

two fowl squawking

two wiggling wrestlers

a walnut on a wall

X x

ax

A fox and an ox are mixing
alphabet soup in a box.
It is an excellent exercise.

exhaust

There are exactly
six saxophone players
in the taxi.

Yak is playing
with his yo-yo.

Y y

Why is the roly-poly pig
crying? He has his own toy.

yacht

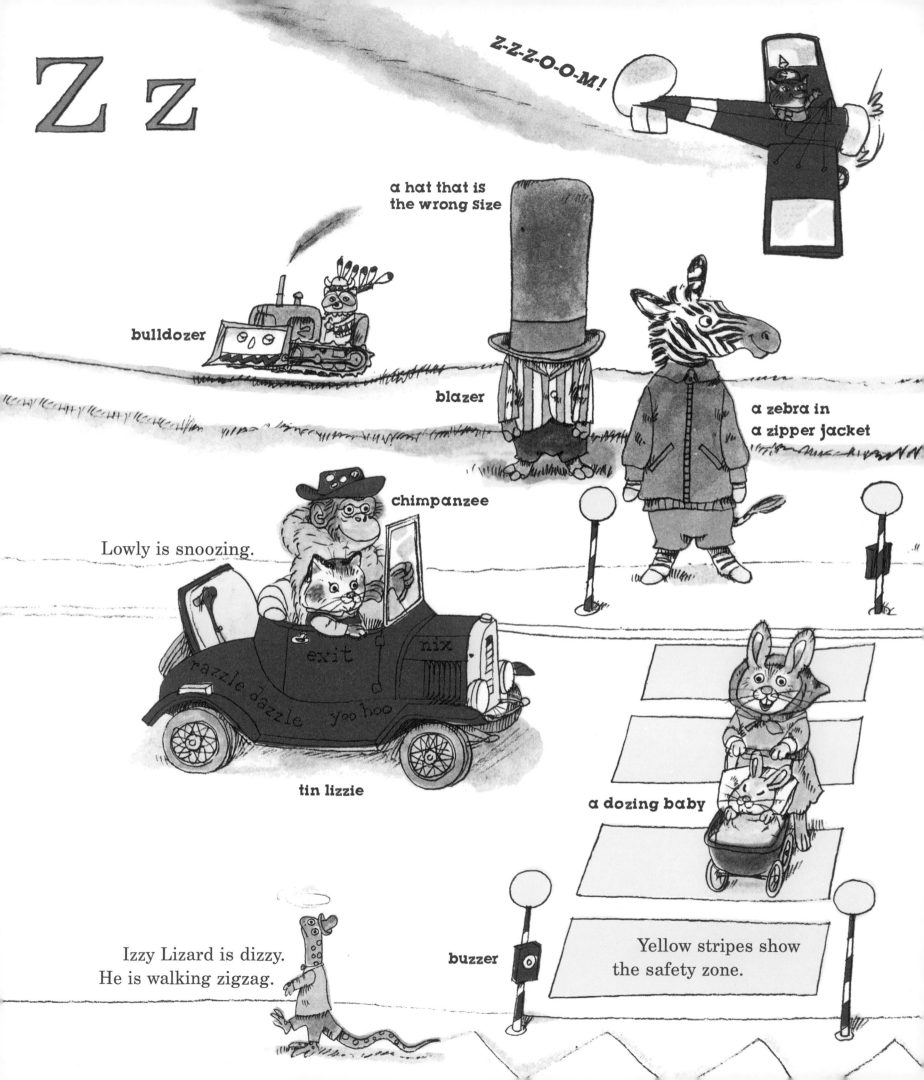

Z z

Z-Z-Z-O-O-M!

a hat that is the wrong size

bulldozer

blazer

a zebra in a zipper jacket

chimpanzee

Lowly is snoozing.

razzle dazzle   exit   nix   yoo hoo

tin lizzie

a dozing baby

Izzy Lizard is dizzy. He is walking zigzag.

buzzer

Yellow stripes show the safety zone.

a b c